Bantam Books in the Choose Your Own Adventure™ Series
Ask your bookseller for the books you have missed

INSIDE *UFO* *54-40*

BY EDWARD PACKARD

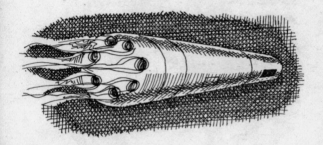

ILLUSTRATED BY PAUL GRANGER

BANTAM BOOKS
TORONTO · NEW YORK · LONDON · SYDNEY

RL 4, IL age 10 and up

INSIDE UFO 54-40
A Bantam Book / February 1982

CHOOSE YOUR OWN ADVENTURE ™
is a trademark of Bantam Books, Inc.

Illustrated by Paul Granger

ISBN 0-553-20197-2

Published simultaneously in the United States and Canada

Bantam Books are published by Bantam Books, Inc. Its trade-
mark, consisting of the words "Bantam Books" and the por-
trayal of a rooster, is Registered in U.S. Patent and Trademark
Office and in other countries. Marca Registrada. Bantam
Books, Inc., 666 Fifth Avenue, New York, New York 10103.

PRINTED IN THE UNITED STATES OF AMERICA

0 9 8 7 6 5 4 3

WARNING!!!!

Do not read this book straight through from beginning to end! These pages contain many different adventures you can have inside *UFO 54-40*. From time to time as you read along, you will be asked to make a choice. Your choice may lead to success or disaster! The adventures you have will be the result of the decisions you make. After you make your choice, follow the instructions to see what happens to you next.

SPECIAL WARNING!!!!

While you are on board *UFO 54-40*, you may hear about *Ultima*, the planet of paradise, and you may wonder if one of your adventures will lead you there.

Sad to say, many never reach *Ultima*, because no one can get there by making choices or following instructions!

There *is* a way to reach *Ultima*. Maybe you'll find it.

ᕬ GS RAKMA ᕬ

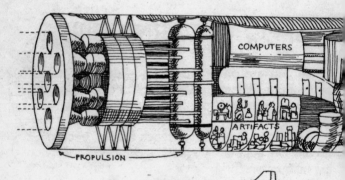

PROPULSION

COMPUTERS

ARTIFACTS

CONCORDE: FOR COMPARISON

INSIDE *UFO*
54-40

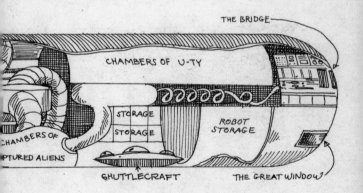

THE BRIDGE

CHAMBERS OF U-TY

STORAGE

STORAGE

ROBOT STORAGE

CHAMBERS OF CAPTURED ALIENS

SHUTTLECRAFT

THE GREAT WINDOW

It's your first trip on the Concorde, the super-sonic jet airliner that crosses the Atlantic in three hours and forty-five minutes. Right now you're at 57,000 feet, in mid-flight from New York to Paris. You look up from the magazine you've been reading as a voice comes over the loudspeaker.

"This is Captain Ravel speaking. We're about halfway across the Atlantic now—at latitude 54, longitude 40. We've just come onto a new course that will bring us over the coast of France in about ninety minutes. Those of you on the left side of the plane may be able to see the southern tip of Greenland . . ."

You glance out of the window, hoping to see

Greenland. Instead, you see a gleaming white cylinder, several times larger than the Concorde, but without wings, engines, or ports. The object, glistening in the early morning sunlight, is coming straight at you!

"Look!"

The white-haired man sitting next to you leans toward the window to get a better view. "At what?"

"Don't you see it? It's coming right at us!"

He opens his mouth to answer, but says nothing, because you are no longer there. . . .

Turn to page 6.

Though there is no one in the room, you speak out in a loud voice. "Return me to Earth! You have no right to hold me prisoner!"

THE ONLY LAW IS THE LAW OF THE U-TY.

Again, the voice seems to be inside your brain. When it speaks this time, a whole wall dissolves before your eyes. A moment later you find yourself floating through the air, drawn by some mysterious force along a curving passageway. In the dim yellow light you can make out human figures. Sitting right in front of you, on thin white mats, are a girl with long black hair and a slender blond boy. Their legs are crossed, and their arms are folded in front of them. They seem to be meditating.

You are excited to find other human beings, yet you suddenly feel very tired. You want to sleep. Maybe you'll be able to think better when you wake up. . . .

If you lie down to sleep, turn to page 5.

If you fight off the urge to sleep and try to wake up the others, turn to page 16.

If you decide to explore elsewhere, turn to page 8.

"Tell me more about yourselves," you say. "Why did you choose to visit Earth?"

WE STUDY EARTH PEOPLE AS YOUR SCIENTISTS STUDY BACTERIA UNDER A MICROSCOPE. WE CAME TO EARTH IN SEARCH OF *ULTIMA*—THE PLANET OF PARADISE.

If you offer to help the U-TY masters find Ultima, *turn to page 22.*

If you ask the U-TY how they think they could reach Ultima *by visiting Earth, turn to page 25.*

The moment you lie down, you fall asleep. Thoughts stream through your unconscious mind. . . .

WHEN YOU ARE HAPPY
YOU WILL BE GOOD.
YOU WILL BE HAPPY
WHEN YOU ARE GOOD.

You sit up. Something is in your hair. *There is a band around your head.* It feels hard to the touch, yet strangely comfortable. *What is it?* Does it have something to do with the strange thoughts running through your head?

As you start to pull off the band, you feel a sharp pain in your head. When you take your hand away, you feel as happy and contented as you have ever been.

If you still try to take the band off your head, turn to page 11.

If you decide to leave it on for a while and see what happens, turn to page 14.

6

You are sitting on a thick, rubbery mat in a circular room. The room is bathed in a pale, white light, yet you see no windows or doors or lamps. You remember now—sitting in the Concorde . . . the huge white object coming at you . . . the plane shuddering, and . . . *where are you?*

The pale light turns violet, and, mixing with oranges and reds, it brightens, as if the sun were about to rise. A voice is speaking—except it is not speaking. *You are hearing thoughts entering directly into your brain!*

WE ARE THE U-TY MASTERS. YOU ARE ON THE GALACTIC SHIP *RAKMA*, ORBITING THE PLANET EARTH. YOU HAVE BEEN CHOSEN TO BE A SPECIMEN IN THE GALACTIC ZOO ON THE IMPERIAL PLANET OF RA. IF YOU REFUSE TO COOPERATE, YOU WILL BE SENT TO SOMO. YOU MAY MAKE ONE STATEMENT.

*If you demand to be returned to Earth,
turn to page 3.*

*If you want to know more about the U-TY,
turn to page 4.*

You grope along the wall of the cavern-like chamber, seeking a door or a passageway to another part of the ship. What do the U-TY masters want of you? Why did they have to pick *you*—out of four billion people in the world?

YOU SHALL NOT LEAVE THE CHAMBER OF THE EARTH PEOPLE.

Once again, the voice you hear is not a voice at all, but a thought directly entering your brain.

"Press against the wall on your left." This time another voice is speaking—a real voice! You cautiously touch the wall. Instantly, it dissolves. There, hovering in the air, is a blue-gray form, shaped like a human, but fuzzy and indistinct—like a patch of very thick fog.

"You can help us." The creature speaks from somewhere within its vaporous, mouthless head. "My name is Incu, captive from Alara."

"How do you know my language?" you ask.

"Think how much you can learn in 800 Earth years. . . . That's how long I've been a prisoner on this ship."

"How could I help?" you ask. "I have no power."

Go on to page 10.

Incu holds out a tiny statue. "It has taken me hundreds of years to make this. It is an idol that the U-TY masters—the rulers of this ship—believe will lead them to *Ultima*, the planet of paradise. They will follow the orders of whomever holds it, *if* that person is a human being. I am not, but *you* are—so take it. But you must promise me this: if you get control of this ship, you will take me to my home planet!"

You think a moment and say, "Before I decide to promise you anything, tell me, would *I* be able to reach *Ultima*?"

"You can not reach it by choosing what to do," says Incu.

Before you can ask him what he means, you hear the voice inside your brain. . . .

FOLLOW THE AMBER LIGHTS BACK TO THE CHAMBER OF THE EARTH PEOPLE. DO NOT TALK. DO NOT TAKE ANYTHING WITH YOU.

"*GO*, and take this—*but only if you will keep your promise.*" Incu presses the idol toward you.

If you take the idol, turn to page 15.

If you leave the idol with Incu, turn to page 18.

You rip off the band, but your head is instantly wracked with a terrible, blinding pain. You throw the band across the chamber. The pain eases. You can see again.

If only you could find a way to escape! Wailing musical sounds fill your ears. The wall at the far end of the chamber dissolves into thin air. You see a long passageway ahead. You run down it. You see a whirling gray figure ahead of you—an alien! Could it be trying to escape too? It swoops into a narrow tunnel. You follow as fast as you can.

At the far end of the tunnel, you see a silver structure shaped like a giant clam! Could it be a spacecraft? The alien opens a hatch and climbs inside.

Go on to page 12.

This may be your chance! You follow the creature through the hatch. Inside, you find the alien is just a few feet away from you. It looks like a big, half-deflated ball, but with rows of eyes and mouths that remind you of portholes on a ship. It must have at least seven or eight legs, with branches, or roots, some of which seem to serve as arms, hands, flippers and antennae.

You watch in amazement as the alien touches various instruments with its many-tentacled "arms." Then it turns some of its eyes on you.

"You're an Earthling, aren't you?" The creature speaks from the mouth closest to you.

"Yes, I am," you stammer. "Who are you?"

"Call me Mopo. This is my last chance to escape, and there's only one place for me to go."

Before he can continue, the hatch closes, and you feel a jolt so violent that you go out like a light.

Turn to page 111.

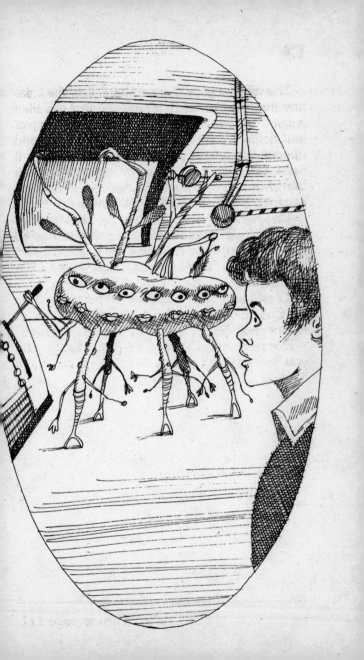

14

It must be a good thing, wearing the band. You soon feel better than ever before, as if you were sailing on a pink cloud . . . except you wonder, just a bit, whether you made the right decision, though you don't think much more about it, because the sun must have set on your pink cloud, for the edges are turning darker. . . . As you slip into the night—dreaming that you are drifting through time—*faster now, whirling faster through time, then slowing, drifting less fast, more slowly through time, now dreaming more slowly, more slowly still . . . until . . . time . . . stops.*

The End

You take the idol and start down the passage-way, following the moving amber lights. The object in your hand seems to be a statue of a human head—a strangely distorted head.

Suddenly the lights grow brighter. You can see the idol more clearly. It looks like one of the mysterious stone statues erected in ancient times by the inhabitants of Easter Island, in the South Pacific. But you have no chance to think further. The voice of the U-TY sounds in your brain.

LIE DOWN AND SLEEP NOW.

You want to resist, but you feel drowsy, very drowsy. You lie down and doze off, wondering—what good is this idol? What powers does it have? How will it get you home?

Turn to page 54.

You shake the boy. He stirs, opens an eye and then slowly gets to his feet.

"My name is Ingmar," he says. "I'm glad to see you. You're the first new Earth person in over fifty years. How were you captured?"

"I was on an airplane, and I saw this huge spaceship coming, and then, somehow, they took me aboard."

"It was the same with me," says Ingmar. "Only it happened more than three centuries ago, long before airplanes were invented on Earth. I was working on my father's farm in Sweden. There was a tremendous thunder-and-lightning storm. I ran for the barn. The next thing I knew—*here I was!*"

"Three hundred years! Has anyone escaped in all that time?" you ask.

Ingmar puts a hand on your shoulder. "I'm afraid not. This ship is controlled by the U-TY masters. They collect specimens of the most intelligent species in the galaxy. This is the chamber of the Earth people. Other chambers contain creatures from other planets."

Go on to the next page.

"Is there any way to see the rest of the ship?"

"Sometimes we can move about, but we can never be sure when. You may find that you can do things here with your mind that you could only do with your hands on Earth. Or, if you have the right kind of mind, and you stand by the forward wall, and you think hard enough, you may gain entrance to the chamber beyond it. But what would happen to you, I cannot say. I have never been willing to take the chance."

If you try to get to the next chamber, turn to page 30.

If you try to wake up the girl, turn to page 32.

You leave Incu and his idol and follow the small amber lights that float ahead, guiding you along the long, curving passageway. Purple-tinted white walls arch around you like the interior of an enormous sea shell. The passageway spirals upward and broadens into a circular room. There, hovering in air, is another alien, the size of a small bear. Its oval head looks like an enormous egg standing on end, and its body seems to be nothing more than the joining point for four tentacle-arms and four spiny legs. It has huge green eyes, almost no nose, and a long expressive mouth that extends almost from the top to the bottom of its hard, shiny face.

As you shrink back, the creature laughs. "You're one of us!" it says. "My name is Qally." The creature holds out a tentacle. Cautiously, you allow it to take your hand in its warm, rubbery grip.

"What planet were you collected from, Qally?"

"The planet Karim of the star Akbar—thirty-eight light-years from your planet Earth."

Go on to the next page.

"Do you know what they plan to do with us?"

Speaking in a low voice, as if afraid of being overheard, Qally says, "The rulers of this ship—the U-TY—have been investigating Earth for hundreds of years, for they believed that Earth was the key to reaching the sublime planet of *Ultima*. Now they have decided to look elsewhere. In only a few days the *Rakma* will leave this solar system, and you and I and all the other captives will be placed in the zoo on the imperial planet of Ra."

"Then is there any way I can escape to Earth?" you ask.

Qally is silent for a moment. Then he says, "I can not promise anything, but I can show you the way to the forbidden chamber. I don't know what's there, but it has something to do with *time*. I would not dare go there, but it could be your only chance."

*If you decide to go to the forbidden chamber,
turn to page 34.*

*If you try to find some other way to escape,
turn to page 36.*

You tell Mopo not to worry—that he can trust human beings. "Let's get out of the water," he shouts. The fishermen throw you a rope and pull you aboard. Then Mopo leaps out of the water and lands on the deck.

The grizzle-faced captain steps forward, his eyes fixed on the alien. "I've seen a lot of strange creatures in the sea, but nothing like you—and you even talk! You may be the devil for all I know, but I don't see that you mean any harm, so you'll be as well treated on this ship as any ship-wrecked sailor. Follow me."

The captain shows you into the deck house. Mopo follows, scuttling like a crab crawling along the beach. The fishermen watch in amazement.

The captain pours you a cup of hot chocolate, but his eyes hardly leave the alien creature beside you. "Would you like something to eat?" he asks Mopo.

"No," Mopo says, "I ate a few months ago."

The captain smiles, shakes his head, and turns toward you. "We're bound for Seattle, with a cargo of tuna. We'll be there in forty-eight hours. Do you think I should notify the Coast Guard about this? They'll never believe me."

If you ask the captain to notify the Coast Guard at once, turn to page 57.

If you suggest keeping the news quiet until you reach Seattle, turn to page 58.

"I can't promise that you will be treated well," you say to Mopo. "Some Earth people might want to harm you."

You interrupt yourself to catch a rope thrown from the ship as Mopo calls, "I am your friend." You turn to answer, but only in time to see him dive beneath the waves.

Two fishermen pull you aboard. Others lean over the rail, looking for the alien.

"What was that?" "Was it a sea lion?" "That was the weirdest thing I ever saw!" They are all talking at once. When you tell them that the creature was an alien life form, most of them shake their heads in disbelief.

A few days later, when you reach home, your family and friends are relieved to see you alive and well. They are eager to hear of your adventure. But when you tell them everything that happened, not one of them believes your story.

In the years ahead you hear about fishermen who claim to have seen a strange creature with rows of eyes and mouths. Some of them say it's a monster which has survived from prehistoric times. Others say it's as friendly as a dolphin. You are glad to know that Mopo is alive. You hope that somehow, someday, you'll see him again.

The End

"I will help you find the way to *Ultima*," you say.

YOU WANT TO HELP US. THAT IS GOOD. NOW YOU WILL GO TO THE CHAMBER OF EARTH PEOPLE.

You are pulled—as if by an invisible magnet—through a long curving passageway that leads to an enormous room. At least a dozen people are there—seated in sleek chairs or on floor cushions. You see a sailor, a woman wearing a gown with stripes of different colors, a man dressed as a samurai warrior, and a beautiful olive-skinned woman whose dark hair flows over her shoulders and reaches her waist.

The samurai warrior walks over to you and bows. "Welcome to the Chamber of Earth People. Like you, we are all captives of the U-TY masters."

"How long have you been here?"

"Six hundred years—since the time of Yoshimitsu, Shogun of Japan. In that time I've learned a great deal about the universe and about Earth—including your language."

"You don't grow old here?"

"No. The U-TY masters have kept us at the age we were when we were captured."

Go on to the next page.

You look around. Some of the people are reading; others are watching a video machine. A girl about your age is playing the flute. It sounds beautiful, and you wonder if she has been practicing for hundreds of years.

Next you notice an old man with long white hair and twinkling blue eyes. His face has a serene expression, and you imagine that he must be very wise.

A girl with long black hair, and a blond boy sit in another corner. Their legs are crossed and their

Go on to page 24.

arms are folded in front of them. They both seem to be in trances, but, as you look at them, the girl smiles, as if she had been expecting you. "I'm Kim Lee," she says.

If you talk to the wise-looking old man, turn to page 37.

If you talk to Kim Lee, turn to page 117.

"How could you find *Ultima* by visiting Earth?" you ask.

The moment you speak, sparks fly about your head, buzzing like angry bees. You dive to the floor, and cover your face with your arms. The sparks die down, except for a glowing ember that lands near your feet. It flares for a few seconds, then turns gray, then black. Cautiously, you touch it and then pick it up. It's like a tiny smooth pebble you might find on the beach, yet it's *denser than lead!*

YOU WILL COOPERATE.

The voice is speaking again. Trying to gather your wits, you answer, "I am a human being. Please . . ."

The lights flicker. The ship is descending so fast that you are pinned to the floor.

YOU ARE UNSUITABLE. WE SHALL RE-TURN YOU TO EARTH. YOUR MEMORY WILL BE ERASED. YOU WILL NEVER KNOW THAT YOU HAVE BEEN IN SPACE.

Turn to page 114.

You check with the computer. The ship has steadied on course for Alara. You can hardly believe it. First you were a helpless prisoner. Now you are in control of a galactic spaceship!

During the long voyage to Alara, you learn about the strange and wonderful alien life forms on board. The U-TY have made millions of video recordings of life on Earth. You learn how to retrieve them from the computer, and spend much of your time watching them on three dimensional playback. You see movies and plays, witness all the battles, the adventures, and great events of human history, and learn far more about Earth life than you would in any school in the world.

You worry about losing so many years of your life. But you know that the U-TY have many powers. So you order them to keep you from growing any older. From then on you feel better knowing that, though you will have to spend thirty-two more years in space, you will return to Earth with your whole life ahead of you—with knowledge of the universe possessed by no human being who ever lived.

The End

Holding the idol in your outstretched hand, you command the U-TY, "Take this ship to the planet Earth!"

IT SHALL BE DONE. TIME TO EARTH ORBIT—THIRTEEN DAYS.

You return to Incu. "I'm sorry I can't take you to your home planet, but I'm sure you would be welcomed on Earth."

"Perhaps," says Incu, "but my body would not hold together in the strong winds that blow on your planet."

"Are you sure there is no way we can get to *Ultima*, the planet of paradise?" you ask.

"Not by any choice you could make," says Incu.

"Then, as soon as the U-TY let me off on Earth, I will direct them to take you to Alara. That won't be too difficult for them to do, will it?"

"I'm afraid it will be," Incu replies. "Once you leave this ship, the U-TY will imprison me and take me to the zoo on the imperial planet of Ra."

"I'm sorry. . . ." You turn toward the great window and stare out at the star-studded blackness of space.

Turn to page 112.

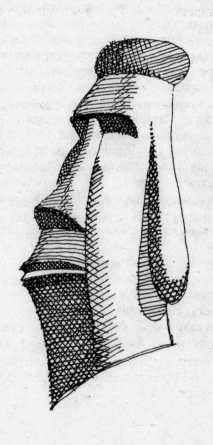

You stand for a long time staring at the forward wall, thinking about it as hard as you can. You begin to feel dizzy, yet you keep concentrating on the wall. Then, without seeming to have been asleep, you feel as if you are awakening. Somehow you find yourself in another chamber, one with a long, curved window. Looking out into space, you see an enormous blue-white disc—*Earth*! Then, turning, you see an alien—a furry creature hardly more than half your size. It is floating in the air—somehow free of the artificial gravity which keeps your feet on the floor.

"Do not be afraid," says the creature. "My name is Bru—a captive from Planet Six of the star Abbar."

"Are there others here from your planet?" you ask.

"I am the only one, and soon there will be none, because I am about to escape to the nearest planet—Earth!"

"Could I come with you?"

"You may if you wish. But, if we fail, the U-TY will place us in Somo—to sleep for a billion years."

If you want to risk it, turn to page 48.

If you say, "I don't want to risk being sent to Somo," turn to page 49.

You touch the girl. She stirs, then sits up, rubbing her eyes. She looks at you curiously for a moment, then says, "I'm glad you're here. I'm Kim Lee."

"You know my language?"

Kim Lee stands up, stretches and looks intently into your eyes. "Language is no problem here. We have hundreds of years to learn."

"You're hundreds of years old?"

"I was collected 475 years ago, during the reign of the Emperor Cheng-te. I was a princess, but here that means nothing."

"But you look only a few years older than I do!"

Kim Lee smiles. "The U-TY masters stopped our aging process, so I have not grown up. But I have learned more than I would in a dozen lifetimes on Earth."

"How long have you been sleeping?"

"It was just a short nap—about twenty-five Earth days."

"Twenty-five Earth days?"

Turn to page 117.

Qally points to a wall at the forward end of the chamber. "Press against that wall, and you'll be able to walk right through it. Good luck!"

You press against the wall. It yields to the weight of your body as though made of cotton. You pass through, and it forms again behind you, as solid and smooth as steel.

"Sit down, or you may fall over," a voice says.

You look around, but to your amazement there is no one in the room except a small child, hardly more than a baby. You sit next to the child and gaze into his large brown eyes.

"You're just a baby," you say, "yet you can talk. You must be older than you look."

"I was once a full-grown man," the baby replies. "This is the time-reversal chamber—the U-TY's greatest invention. Here, time runs backward. In eighteen months I will no longer exist—because I will not yet have been born."

"Does that mean that now I'll grow younger too?"

"Indeed, you are right now," the baby replies. "However old you are—that's how long it will be until you're born. I will be born much sooner than you. Then you will be all alone."

Go on to the next page.

"What will happen to you after you are born?"

"I will not exist."

"How awful."

"I suppose so," the baby says, "but it will be no worse for me than it was for you before *you* were born. There's always a chance that my life will start again sometime in the past. Maybe I will become my father, and then, when he is born, I will become *his* father!"

"Is there no way out of here?" you ask.

"None—except—you could try walking through that portal. But, if you try, you may be for a moment in two times at the same place, or, what is worse, two places at the same time!"

If you risk escape, turn to page 40.

If you decide to stay and hope for a better chance to escape, turn to page 51.

"Qally," you say, "are you sure there's no other way to escape?"

"If only Earth people could control their thoughts . . . then you'd have a chance."

"How do you mean?"

"Before leaving your planet," says Qally, "the U-TY plan to take treasures from one of the greatest museums in your world—the Metropolitan Museum of Art in New York. The police will come, but the U-TY only need a few minutes to collect what they need."

"What would happen if the police shot at the U-TY?"

"They have evolved so that matter gets out of their way. If you lit a fire under one of the U-TY, its form would be transposed, so that instead of being burned by the fire, it would gather energy from it! Although they are in no danger, they might want to use you as a decoy—to distract the guards. If you volunteer to help, they might ask you to go with them. Once you're on Earth, you'll have a chance to escape. But I don't see how you could succeed, because *if, while talking to them, you think even once of how you want to escape, they will read your mind and send you to Somo— the chamber where they put you to sleep for a billion years.*"

If you take a chance on being able to control your thoughts while offering to help the U-TY, turn to page 52.

If you decide to look for another way to escape, turn to page 65.

"Pardon me, sir," you say to the old man. "Can you tell me about the U-TY masters—who they are, and what they will do with us?"

For a moment, the old man seems lost in thought. Then, looking you in the eye, he lays a wrinkled hand on your shoulder. "You came to the right person. My name is Angus. I was the first human captured by the U-TY—aliens advanced so far beyond Earth people that they are made of energy instead of matter. That was almost 1200 years ago—the same year the Vikings invaded Scotland. I can tell you what you want to know. But knowledge does not always bring happiness. I think you should wait before asking me. We have lots of time."

If you decide to wait, turn to page 61.

If you ask the old man to tell you everything now, turn to page 64.

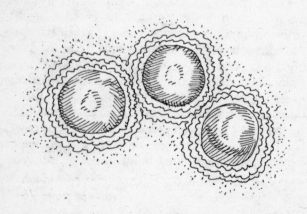

38

"Follow me," Kim Lee says. "We will find the U-TY. But remember, if we say the wrong thing, they will store us forever, like eggs in a carton."

Your new friend leads you through a series of long, twisting corridors. Sometimes you pass through walls that dissolve at her touch and then form again behind you. Suddenly, the U-TY masters are before you—three spheres no larger than basketballs! They hover in the air, glowing like pink and violet clouds above the setting sun.

What will they do? What will they ask? At first, nothing happens. You want to speak, but you dare not. Are you being hypnotized by the glowing pulsing lights? For a moment you wonder whether you are still alive, or whether you have entered an after-life of another universe. . . .

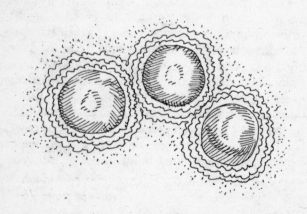

Go on to the next page.

The voices, rich as a chord played on an organ, sound in your brain.

WE HAVE BEEN WATCHING YOU. WE CAN PREDICT EVERYTHING YOU WILL EVER DO, EVER SAY, FOR THE REST OF YOUR LIFE.

On hearing these words you are filled with anger and fear. You try to think of something that would truly surprise them.

If you cry, "PUT ME BACK ON EARTH!"
turn to page 75.

If you throw back your head and laugh,
turn to page 76.

If you say two lines from a nursery rhyme,
thinking that they never could predict that you
would say that, turn to page 79.

You fling yourself through the portal, hoping to get through fast enough to avoid being in the two places at once. But as your legs run forward, your head and shoulders are wrenched behind you. In a whirlpool of time, moving backward, and at the same time forward, you are swept into eternity.

The End

You miss the wastebasket, and the object bangs against the wall. As you reach to pick it up, it leaps out of your hand and buzzes around your head like an angry bee. Then, while you stand dumbfounded, the object spins through your bedroom window, leaving only a tiny hole in the glass.

You touch the hole. It feels as smooth as the rim of a drinking glass. Suddenly you remember the sparks flying about your head. *You were on a UFO!*

You rush toward the door to tell whomever is home, then stop short and think for a minute: your whole adventure might as well have been a dream, for who will believe it?

The End

You give the U-TY the order to reverse course and head for Alara. The main computer begins to vibrate as the ship slowly arcs on to a new course. As you stand before the controls, you are overcome by gloom—you have sentenced yourself to thirty-two years in this prison. The thought of it is like a heavy weight in your chest.

Why should you sacrifice yourself just so Incu can get home? Why not reverse course yet again, and head for Earth?

Still, you are concerned about what the U-TY would think of you if you kept changing your mind.

On the other hand, you don't want to stay in space for years and years—you want to go home!

If you decide it's best to continue on toward Alara, turn to page 27.

If you order the U-TY to reverse course again and head for Earth, turn to page 99.

Each day you enjoy watching the Earth grow larger on the vision screen, but you feel bad about Incu; he is growing thinner and thinner, like a patch of fog in the morning sun.

One day, as you are watching the Earth, marveling at its coat of swirling white clouds, the deceleration lights start flashing. *"Take re-entry stations,"* the computer calls out. *"Prepare to enter Earth atmosphere in eight minutes."*

You must tell the U-TY where they should land on Earth! Holding the power-giving idol in one hand, you call out, "Land in the United States. Obtain landing instructions from the U.S. Air Force."

But the computer quickly answers, *"Your last transmission is in error. You wish to land on the Island of the Gods."*

What has happened? Why doesn't the computer obey orders? Should you insist on landing in the United States and risk trouble with the computer? On the other hand, the "Island of the Gods" is somewhere on Earth, and you could figure out how to get home from wherever it is.

If you let the computer land the ship on the "Island of the Gods," turn to page 44.

If you insist on landing in the United States, turn to page 46.

"Proceed to the Island of the Gods."

The computer responds, and for the next half-hour you watch the Earth passing below you as the ship glides smoothly and silently toward the surface.

The moment the ship lands, you step out of the deceleration chamber and direct the computer to open the ports. A panel slides open. You step through a hatchway and jump down to the rocky soil of Earth. Squinting in the brilliant sunlight, you find yourself looking at a weird yet familiar scene. You are on Easter Island, in the South Pacific.

Turning your back to the blustery wind, you contemplate the melancholy landscape. The barren hillside before you is strewn with massive stone statues, fifteen to twenty feet high. They are shaped like the tiny statue you still hold in your hand. Why have the U-TY landed you here? Is this what they meant by the Island of the Gods? What do they expect to find here?

As you ponder these questions, the voice of the U-TY speaks.

IT IS WRITTEN IN THE ANCIENT LAWS THAT WHEN A HUMAN SHOWS THE IDOL OF THE GODS TO THE U-TY, THE U-TY SHALL FIND THE PATH TO *ULTIMA*, THE PLANET OF PARADISE.

Turn to page 71.

You tell the U-TY they must land in the United States. The ship breaks out of orbit and descends with frightening speed. Pressed against the contoured wall of the acceleration chamber, you feel as if you weigh a thousand pounds! Something is very wrong! Why aren't the alarms sounding?

"What's happening?" you ask the computer.

"PROGRAMMING PARADOX. INCONSISTENT TRUTHS."

Through the viewer you can see the Earth rushing up to meet you. The ship can hardly be more than ten miles above the surface!

"Stop!" Flattened by extreme gravity forces, you are hardly able to open your mouth as you cry out, *"Return to orbit . . . set course for Island of Gods. . . ."*

Now, even as the computer is attempting to reverse course, violent forces are crushing your body. You are traveling at sixteen miles per second. There isn't time. . . .

Go on to the next page.

Forty minutes later, an aide reports to the President of the United States—"We have reports of the impact of a large meteorite in western Nebraska. It made a crater a hundred yards wide. The explosion shattered windows twenty miles away. Fortunately, no one was injured, as far as we know."

The End

"I'll risk it!" you say.

"Then we have no time to lose," Bru says. "Follow me."

Bru leads you through a series of narrow, winding passageways. He stops at a wall that looks no different from any of the others.

"Beyond this wall is the space shuttle," says Bru. "Usually, only the U-TY masters can dissolve it, but I think I can do it now."

"Why now?"

"The U-TY have lowered the force field, because their robots are preparing for a final trip to Earth before their ship leaves this solar system forever."

Bru floats before the wall; slowly, it begins to dissolve. A moment later the two of you pass through into a brightly lit chamber. Before you is the gleaming white shuttlecraft.

"They use this vehicle to collect their samples from Earth," Bru says.

As he speaks, the wall forms again, sealing the passageway behind you. Bru opens the latch and floats inside the craft. You are right behind him. In a moment you hear a rumbling and then a rushing of air. *Blast off!* Your head aches. Sweat pours off your body. The force increases unbearably. A moment later you are unconscious.

Turn to page 113.

You tell Bru that you don't want to try to escape right now. He seems disappointed, and floats away without saying anything. He returns a few hours later. There is a sad look in his eyes.

"Will there be another chance for escape?" you ask.

"It's too late," Bru says. "We've left Earth's orbit, and even the solar system. We're bound for Galaxy 32.9, Planet 6.3, star 149, Omega Cluster."

Turning toward the great window, you gaze through your tears into endless black space. You realize that you will never see home again.

The End

The strange object lands in the wastebasket with a thud, and you think no more about it.

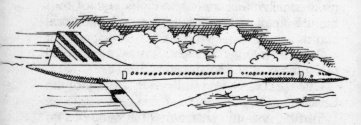

A few days later you are talking with a friend of yours, Todd Hawkins.

"Did you see the airline pilot on TV last night?" Todd asks. "He and his crew swear that a couple of days ago they saw an alien space ship over the Atlantic."

"Really?"

"Yeah; it was at latitude 54, longitude 40, so they've called it *UFO 54-40*. At first they thought a passenger was missing, but none of the doors had opened—there was no way a passenger could have disappeared. They finally decided that the passenger list must have been wrong."

Something about what Todd tells you sets you to thinking about that flight you took on the Concorde, and something about a trip to France, but for some reason, no matter how hard you try, you just can't remember what happened.

The End

Life is pleasant in the reversal chamber. There is much to learn and do—games, video screens, computers . . . but each day you watch the baby grow smaller and smaller. At the age of four months it can no longer talk; its mouth and vocal chords are no longer sufficiently developed. For awhile, it gestures helplessly; then it can only thrash around like a new-born baby.

One day the U-TY robots come and place the baby in a glass-walled box. The box is like an incubator, and you realize that the baby has no longer been born. Now it must have the special protection it would have inside a mother's womb.

For nine months the baby grows smaller and smaller, until one day, the robots remove the empty incubator.

What could have happened to it? Is it growing again in another universe? If so, is it the same person or someone else?

Now you are totally alone, aware that each day you are growing smaller and younger. The day is coming when you, too, will not yet have been born. Then you will no longer exist. You can only hope that at some time in the past you will die once more, and so begin life again.

The End

"I'll take the chance," you say. "I'll try to control my thoughts."

"Then I wish you good luck. Follow me."

Qally shows you the way through a maze of passageways. Finally you reach an area so dark that you can barely see. You feel Qally's tentacles on your shoulder.

"You must continue alone," he says.

You thank Qally for his help and bid him farewell. Then you grope your way along a passageway which presently opens into a round chamber filled with soft, violet-hued light.

Your eyes fasten on the three round objects suspended in the air, glowing with pale violet light like three moons floating in space. As you stand there, almost hypnotized by this vision, you hear their voices sounding inside your brain.

TOMORROW WE LEAVE EARTH ORBIT FOREVER. FIRST, WE SHALL TAKE TREASURES FROM THE METROPOLITAN MUSEUM OF ART. IF YOU DO NOT WISH TO ESCAPE AND WANT TO HELP US REACH *ULTIMA*, YOU SHALL HAVE AN HONORED PLACE AMONG US.

You take a deep breath before replying—"I will help you. I do not wish to escape."

VERY GOOD. WHEN IT IS NEXT MIDNIGHT IN NEW YORK, WE SHALL LAND BEHIND THE METROPOLITAN MUSEUM OF ART. WE SHALL OPEN AN ENTRANCE. OUR ROBOTS WILL TAKE

ART TREASURES. THE GUARDS WON'T BELIEVE WHAT THEY SEE, BECAUSE THEY WILL THINK THAT WHAT THEY SEE IS IMPOSSIBLE. YOU ARE POSSIBLE, BECAUSE YOU ARE AN EARTH PERSON, SO THEY WILL BELIEVE THAT THEY SEE YOU. OUR ROBOTS WILL RESCUE YOU WHEN WE ARE READY TO LEAVE.

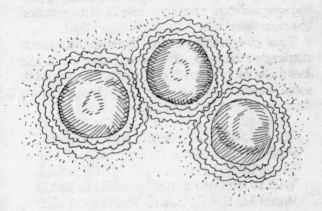

The U-TY rise a few feet in the air and drift toward you. For a moment you tighten up with fear. Then you realize that they only want to touch you. You hold out your hands and feel a tingling sensation as the glowing forms brush against your skin.

A moment later they pass through the walls of the chamber.

Turn to page 82.

You awaken to find yourself in another room. Floating in mid-air are three glowing, pulsating spheres. Your skin tingles; your hair stands on end.

YOU HAVE DISOBEYED THE U-TY. YOU WILL BE SENT TO SOMO TO SLEEP FOR A BILLION YEARS.

So it is these highly charged forms that have been transmitting thoughts into your brain. The U-TY masters!

You hold up the idol and thrust it toward the glowing forms. Instantly they glide toward the floor. Their light dims. The chamber is filled with a low whistling sound.

YOU ARE THE KEY. YOU CAN LEAD US TO *ULTIMA*. COMMAND, AND WE SHALL FOLLOW.

As these words ring inside your brain, you realize the idol *does* have power. The U-TY think that *you* can lead them to *Ultima*, the planet of paradise. You want to ask them to take you to Earth, but you remember that you promised Incu to return him to his home planet.

Go on to page 56.

"How long will it take us to reach Alara?" you ask.

SIXTEEN YEARS.

You feel a sinking feeling. Sixteen years, and sixteen more to return to Earth—thirty-two years on this spaceship! This will be your fate if you keep your promise to Incu.

If you keep your promise to Incu, and order the U-TY to take the space craft to Alara, turn to page 27.

If you decide not to worry about Incu, and order the U-TY to take you directly to Earth, turn to page 28.

The captain radios the Coast Guard. As he predicted, they laugh at his story about picking up an alien creature.

"No matter," he says to you and Mopo, "we'll be in port in two days—then they can see for themselves!"

The next morning you, Mopo, and the captain are standing on the bridge. Resting his arms on the rail, the captain scans the horizon with his binoculars. "If the weather would lift a bit, we could see Mount Rainier from here," he says.

Suddenly a sailor calls from the afterdeck, *"There's a submarine surfacing just off the port quarter. . . . It has . . . a hammer-and-sickle flag!"*

"Russians!" the captain cries.

"They intercepted your message to the Coast Guard," says Mopo.

"I think you're right!" The captain points to the port rail. "They're pulling alongside. They're going to board us!"

"Don't let them capture Mopo!" you cry.

Turn to page 91.

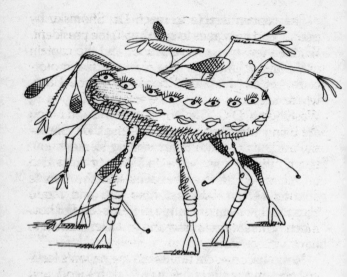

The captain agrees to keep radio silence.

Two days later, the ship steams into Seattle's harbor. You and the captain confer with Mopo.

"While I was held captive by the U-TY, I learned a great deal about your country," says Mopo. "I should speak to the President of the United States as soon as possible. One of your distinguished scientists, Dr. Hubert Shomsky, is an expert on extra-terrestrial life forms. I'm sure I could convince him that I am not a hoax; then he can arrange for me to meet with the president."

Go on to the next page.

The captain is able to reach Dr. Shomsky by phone, and he agrees to speak with the president. Within a few hours, you, Mopo, and the captain are all traveling in a heavily guarded motorcade—headed for McChord Air Force Base, where a special plane is waiting to take you to Washington, D.C. Five hours later you and Mopo are being introduced to the president. Dr. Shomsky and other scientists are waiting to meet you. Later, in a special nationwide TV program carried on all networks, the president tells the people about *UFO 54-40*—and how you and Mopo escaped. He speaks warmly of Mopo, and of how much he has learned from the first alien known to have visited Earth.

Mopo becomes an adviser to the nation's leaders, and, in the years following, it is his work and wisdom more than anything else that help to bring lasting peace to Earth.

The End

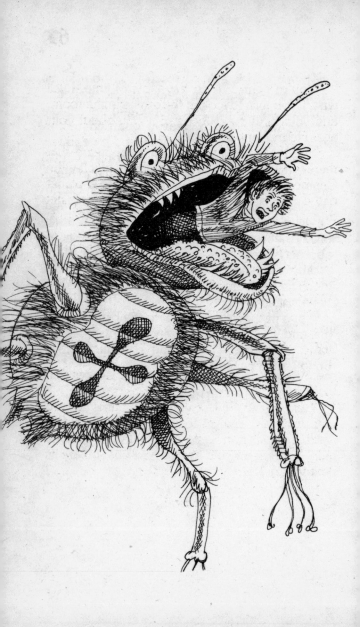

"You're right. We do have lots of time. I will wait." You turn to look at the others in the room, and your eyes meet those of a boy about your age. He motions you over.

"See that wall," he says. "I have heard that there is a way to open it and that behind it lies the Chamber of the Argoni—captives from a planet of the star Denebola. If we could learn how to get through to the Argoni, maybe they could help us escape!"

You tap against the wall. Nothing happens. You kick it as hard as you can. Suddenly it dissolves before your eyes. A long, curving passageway lies before you. The boy starts through it.

You follow cautiously. Looking back you see that the wall has formed again behind you. You continue on through the passageway. The light grows brighter. Now you can see clearly. The room is crowded with huge, hairy creatures that look like great purple-headed spiders.

"Help!" The boy screams and turns toward you. In a flash one of the monsters springs forward. To your horror, it swallows the boy in one gulp! You scream and turn to run, but you are its next victim.

The End

It's not easy to pretend to be crazy. You charge around the room screaming, *"I am Napoleon! I am Napoleon!"*

Nothing happens, but you must keep it up! *"I am Napoleon! I am Napoleon!"* Your voice gets hoarser, and your head aches. You begin to feel as if you really *are* going crazy. Your mind goes blank.

You are lying in a small room. Everything that ever happened to you seems to be far in the past. You must be somewhere in space, for you have no weight at all. A soft voice is speaking in your brain.

YOU WERE ACTING STRANGELY. WE GAVE YOU SOMETHING TO MAKE YOU FEEL CALM AND AT PEACE. YOU ARE UNUSUAL. WE SHALL STUDY YOU CLOSELY . . . IN THE LABORATORIES OF THE U-TY.

The End

"I don't want to wait," you reply. "I want to know the truth now."

"Very well." Angus beckons you closer. "The U-TY have taught us how to speak in thought waves, but we will never understand more than a tenth of what they know. They have studied the Earth for more than one thousand years, hoping to find the path to *Ultima*, the planet of paradise. But they have given up, and are preparing to leave for their home planet, hundreds of light-years away."

"Is there really a planet of paradise?" you ask.

"Yes, there truly is," Angus replies. "But the U-TY have not found it yet, for there is no way to reach *Ultima* by making a choice or following directions."

"Is there any chance I can return to my own home?"

"I wish I knew. I only know that pleading with the U-TY is useless. Perhaps, just perhaps, if you are willing to pretend that you are crazy, they might decide you're unsuitable for the zoo. They might let you go, but I warn you, the U-TY are unpredictable."

Should you pretend to be crazy? The plan might work. On the other hand, the aliens communicate with thought waves. They are highly advanced. Suppose they can tell that you're just pretending. What would they do then?

*If you decide to pretend to be crazy,
turn to page 63.*

If you know you can't, turn to page 107.

"I see what you mean," you say. "I don't think I could keep from thinking about how I want to escape."

You leave Qally and continue to explore the ship, which seems to contain hundreds of chambers and passageways. Each day you explore a different part of the ship, but you can never be sure where you have been before. It is like wandering through a maze where someone is always changing the pattern—sealing some passageways and opening others.

You decide that it would be safer not to confront the U-TY. If you cooperate with them, maybe they will not send you away to Somo.

So, in the weeks ahead, you spend your time looking at some of the videotapes, holograms, and artifacts available to the captives. You find that the U-TY have been observing life on Earth for almost 1400 years. In their records are answers to mysteries of the universe not yet solved by Earth people.

One day you find your way into a large chamber with smooth, curving walls. Suspended in the air are three pale violet shapes. Flickering lines of bright red light play about them like tiny flashes of lightning. For a moment you think you hear them speaking to you.

Go on to page 66.

WE HAVE BEEN WATCHING YOU. YOU HAVE A STRONG SPIRIT WITHIN YOU— SO STRONG THAT YOU ARE DANGEROUS. THIS IS THE LAW. THOSE WHO OBEY THE U-TY WILL BE KEPT IN THE IMPERIAL ZOO ON THE PLANET RA. THOSE WHO RESIST THE U-TY WILL BE SENT TO SOMO AND PUT TO SLEEP FOR A BILLION YEARS. WHAT IS YOUR CHOICE?

You try to think of some logical reply that will keep you from being placed in Somo or the zoo.

If you say, "It is not fair or just to take me from my home or friends, so please return me to the Earth," turn to page 93.

If you say, "I will not obey you, neither will I resist you. Therefore there is no reason to send me to Somo or the zoo," turn to page 118.

Bru stays out of sight while you walk down to the shore.

When you tell the fisherman your story, he looks at you as if you were crazy. You're about to ask him for directions to the nearest town, when a shot rings out, and then another. Looking up, you see Bru floating over your head like a balloon. More shots! Now you see where they're coming from. Two men are driving along the beach in a jeep, and one of them is firing at Bru.

"Stop!" you yell. But Bru is already out of range and rapidly disappearing into the distance.

A heavy-set man jumps out of the jeep. "Hey, did you just see somethin' like a big round ball flying out that way?" He points to the ocean.

"I couldn't believe it!" the driver yells.

You start to speak, but the fisherman steps between you and the jeep. "I don't know what that critter was, but I sure wish you'd gotten it," he says.

You're glad that Bru escaped, but what will become of him? Where will he go? What must he think about Earth people now? You hope he will learn that there are millions and millions of good people on Earth.

The End

You slide down the dune. Bru rolls close behind.

"Hello, there!" you call.

The fisherman stares at you, then steps back and nearly falls as he loses his balance in the soft sand.

"Could you tell us where we are?"

"What's *that*?" The fisherman points at Bru.

"My friend, Bru. He is from another planet."

The fisherman steps closer. "I must be dreaming. This is the most amazing thing I've ever seen."

"Where are we?" you ask again.

"Nags Head, North Carolina. Buck Coleman's my name."

"Do you know how I can get a ride to the White House in Washington, D.C.?" Bru asks. "It could be important for the future of America," he says.

"It's quite a trip, but this sort of thing doesn't happen every day," says Coleman. "Just give me a minute to make a phone call. There's a phone booth right across the road. Now don't go away."

"I guess I'd better call home, too," you tell Bru. "We'll be right back."

"All right," says Bru. "I'll hide in this clump of beach plum trees. I don't want to be spotted until I have a chance to meet with the president."

Go on to page 70.

You try to reach your family, but no one is home. Maybe they think you landed safely in France.

You wait while Coleman talks on the phone. When he hangs up, he has a big grin on his face.

"I just made a deal with some friends of mine who own the local TV station," he says. "All we have to do is stall the alien for about fifteen minutes until they can get here with their cameras, and they'll give us $20,000!" He slaps you on the back. "Half of that is for you, kid—$10,000 all your own!"

"But Bru doesn't want to be seen until he can meet with the president."

"So, it won't hurt him. He'll be a celebrity soon. He might as well learn how America works. Look, all you have to do is not say anything for fifteen minutes, and you've got $10,000!"

You want to respect Bru's wish to avoid publicity, but you didn't make any promises to him. It's hard to see how being on TV would hurt him, and you sure could use $10,000!

*If you agree to Coleman's plan,
turn to page 88.*

*If you insist on telling Bru that the TV crews
are on the way, turn to page 100.*

You can hardly believe the words you hear. Are you dreaming? Yet those cows you see grazing on the hillside are certainly real, and so is that jeep coming up the road, and the large brown-and-white dog barking loudly as it runs toward you.

You watch as the jeep stops, wheels around, and accelerates in the opposite direction, leaving behind a cloud of dust in the wind.

WHAT IS YOUR COMMAND?

The dog is running down the road, tail between its legs. A farmer is kneeling, his hands uplifted in prayer. He must have been terrified by the great space ship that has landed on his island.

You step away from the spacecraft and shout, *"Return to your home planet. Only there will you find the path to Ultima!"*

Almost instantly, the great white cylinder rises into the air. You stand, watching in awe, as it disappears into the clouds.

You are grateful to be back on Earth, and excited by your experience on board a UFO. Your only regret is that you did not keep your promise to Incu.

Walking slowly down the road that will lead you back to civilization, you feel much older than you are.

The End

A half-hour later you are at police headquarters. You are seated at a small wooden table in a dingy room lit by a single bulb overhead. Two officers stand over you. One is a big, swarthy fellow with curly black hair. The other officer is a short, red-faced man. Their badges show that the big one is Lieutenant Fitch; the other, Captain Mackin.

"Well. What's your story?" says Fitch.

"This is going to be hard for you to believe," you say, "but I wasn't in on this. I was captured by aliens in a UFO. They're the ones who took the art . . ."

"Let's not waste time being cute," Mackin interrupts. "You couldn't have been part of a team that stole thirty million dollars worth of art in ten minutes unless you knew exactly what you were doing!"

Fitch lays a heavy hand on your shoulder. "Look, kid, we don't want to send you to jail, but we have to get that art. Come clean and you'll get out of this, but, if you want to make up fairy tales, things will go very hard for you."

"*Very* hard," Mackin adds.

Go on to page 74.

The door flies open. Fitch and Mackin jump to their feet. You can tell that the grim, leather-faced man standing there must be a high-ranking police inspector.

He takes a long look at you and then turns to the others and says, "We've just verified that this was the kid reported missing from Air France Flight 2—the Concorde jet from New York to Paris—and presumed dead!"

"Doesn't look dead to me," Mackin says.

Fitch laughs. "The report *just might be wrong.*"

The Inspector points a cigar at the two officers. "Not according to the CIA and the man I just talked to on the phone—chief of staff to the president. The report is right, but it's being kept secret. We've been ordered to let this kid go with no further questions."

"But . . . what about the art robbery?" asks Mackin.

"It will never be solved," the inspector says. "It's enough for you to know that it's a military secret—at least for now."

The two policemen start to speak. But the Inspector silences them with a wave of his hand. "Your family is on the way to pick you up. I don't think you'll find many people who will believe your story about being captured by aliens from outer space. There will only be a few, like me, who will ever know for sure that you really were inside a UFO."

The End

"Put me back on Earth!"

The moment you speak you fall unconscious. Awakening, you find yourself in a seat that seems strangely familiar. A woman wearing a uniform is standing next to you, her hand on your shoulder. "We're preparing to land. Buckle your seat belt."

You realize that this woman is a stewardess. You are back on the Concorde! Everything is the way it was before . . .

As the stewardess moves down the aisle to check on other passengers, you look dazedly at the white-haired man who was sitting beside you when you were captured. He turns toward you, a surprised look on his face. "Oh, you're back. Where *were* you for such a long time?"

The End

As your laughter echoes through the chamber, the U-TY seem to expand and vibrate. A chorus of voices fills the room.

WE, THE U-TY, WHO ARE ALL-POWERFUL AND ALL-KNOWING, HAVE ORBITED YOUR EARTH LIKE A SILENT, INVISIBLE EYE. WE HAVE SEEN ALL, AND KNOW ALL. ONE THING ONLY WE DO NOT KNOW: WHAT MAKES EARTH PEOPLE LAUGH?

Hearing this, you cannot help but laugh again. A moment ago you were frightened by the awesome presence of the U-TY. Yet now these all-powerful creatures are begging you for the answer to a simple question.

Kim Lee steps forward. "Now, I remember the saying of the Chinese philosopher, Sung Chi—*'If we could not laugh, we could not bear to cry; if we could not cry, we could not bear to live.'*"

"Do you hear the truth, U-TY?" you say loudly, and you repeat Kim Lee's words.

Nothing happens. All is silent. You start to speak again, but Kim Lee touches your arm. "Wait," she whispers.

Go on to page 78.

THE U-TY NEED NOT LAUGH,
THE U-TY NEED NOT CRY.

"Then you are not alive!" you shout the words without thinking.

"NOT ALIVE!" Kim Lee adds her voice to yours.

The U-TY quiver like huge, phosphorescent jellyfish, and their glowing lights brighten, then fade. The rounded walls begin to glow more and more brightly while the air is filled with music of wild winds blowing through organ pipes—rising and falling—then fading as the lights of the U-TY flicker out.

Kim Lee and you look at each other in the dim light. "With all their vast knowledge, they were only dead souls," says Kim Lee. "When they realized that they were not really living, they lost their energy. Since that was all they were made of, they ceased to exist!"

"What will happen to us now?" you ask.

"We must learn to control this UFO. I know how to operate the invisibility screens. Shall I make the ship visible to Earth? That may be our only hope of being rescued."

If you say yes, turn to page 80.

If you say no, turn to page 83.

You think for a moment and say,

Humpty-Dumpty sat on a wall,
Humpty-Dumpty had a great fall,
All the king's horses and all the king's men
Couldn't put Humpty together again.

The U-TY glow more brightly for an instant.

WE KNOW EVERYTHING ABOUT YOU.

You feel like rushing at these cloud-like energy balls, and seizing them. As if to warn you that they know your thoughts, they rise like a shower of sparks, radiating such heat and light that you reel back, throwing up your hands to shield your eyes.

Then you feel a mysterious force pulling you back, lifting your feet off the floor, as the voices call.

WE KNEW THAT YOU WOULD SAY
    THAT RHYME.
NOW WE SHALL GIVE YOU LOTS OF
    TIME.
ON TO SOMO YOU WILL GO
TO SLEEP A BILLION YEARS OR SO.

The End

"Yes. If NASA can see us maybe they can send up a shuttlecraft to bring us down."

Kim Lee leads you to a luminescent panel faced with a complex pattern of shapes and colors. Pointing to a three-dimensional display screen, she says, "Here you can see all the man-made satellites and spacecraft that are above the Earth's atmosphere."

"Earth scientists can see us, too?" you ask.

"Yes. You can imagine they are trying to figure out where this unknown spacecraft came from."

"Do you think we'll be rescued?"

"Either rescued or shot down."

Now there is nothing to do but wait. Fortunately, the computers continue to operate flawlessly, even though the U-TY masters no longer exist. You gaze out at the brilliant moon, then watch Kim Lee experimenting with the controls. She switches on radio traffic from Earth, some in English, some in other languages.

Then, from one of the speakers, a voice calls out, *"We have detected you. We will assume you are an enemy, unless you identify yourself."*

Kim Lee quickly speaks into her microphone. "We are Earth people on a UFO. We have captured it, but cannot control it."

A moment passes. Then the Earth voice again: "Your reply is unacceptable. Reply truthfully or you will be destroyed by laser beams."

You take the microphone from Kim Lee, wondering what you can possibly say to convince them you're telling the truth.

If you say, "I am the person missing from the Concorde. Save us!" turn to page 98.

If you say, "Try to attack us and your whole country will be instantly destroyed," turn to page 90.

The U-TY have just told you of their plan to take treasures from the Metropolitan Museum of Art. You pretended you would help them; but *remember*, they were able to read your mind! While you were with them, *were you able to keep from thinking, even once, about your plan to escape?*

If you couldn't keep from thinking about escaping, turn to page 87.

If you were able to keep from thinking about escaping, turn to page 85.

"No, it's too risky. We'd better stay invisible, at least until we can learn how to fly this ship," you say.

"Yes," Kim Lee replies. "I understand the main controls, but I'm not sure I can safely steer our course."

The two of you study the dozens of strange instruments. "This ship is automated," Kim Lee explains. "You need only feed the computer a general idea of what you want. For instance, this panel is gravity-sensitive. It will cause us to approach the nearest object that has a strong gravitational pull."

"That would be Earth. That's the way we can land!" For the first time you have some hope of returning home safely.

Kim Lee moves her hand along the oblong panel of floating light. A moment later you feel the ship slowly accelerating, and you hear the hum of unseen power. The UFO is descending. The acceleration increases. Your body is pressed against the wall. The force increases still more. It's more than you can bear. You're losing consciousness!

Turn to page 94.

You did it! You were able to keep from thinking about your escape plans!

Soon you are summoned again by the U-TY. They guide you into an automated shuttlecraft, which carries you down through the Earth's atmosphere with incredible speed and smoothness. At 11:50 P.M. you step out onto the Great Lawn near the Metropolitan Museum of Art in New York City. Robots float out of the craft and hover near the wall of the museum. They direct their antennae at the building. A section of the rear wall dissolves. The robots lead you through the hole in the wall. You watch in amazement as they dart about the building, grabbing paintings and statues like bees gathering nectar from flowers.

The alarm sounds. Two guards are running toward you, guns drawn. One of them yells, *"Halt, or I'll shoot!"*

A U-TY robot swoops toward you, but you don't want to be taken back to the ship! You dive onto the floor between the two guards.

The air is split by the sound of a siren.

Go on to page 86.

"Help! Save me!" you yell at the guards.

They step back. One of them has you covered with his revolver, and you stand, shaking, hands in the air. Other guards rush toward you. The U-TY robots are gone. A guard handcuffs you and leads you to the front entrance, while the others run around shouting at each other. Squad cars have already blocked off the Avenue. Half a dozen policemen are running up the broad steps leading up from the sidewalk. Others are headed around the sides of the building.

Turn to page 73.

You realize that you could not keep yourself from thinking about your escape plan. The U-TY may have read your thoughts. They have left you in darkness. Now you stand alone, waiting, wondering what your fate will be.

Soon you feel yourself being slowly pulled as if by some magnetic force. Then, in the dim amber light, you see that you are in a vast chamber that is filled as far as the eye can see with all kinds of creatures, human and inhuman. They are all floating in space, seemingly deep in sleep.

YOU ARE ENTERING SOMO.

The U-TY really did read your mind. They knew that you wanted to escape. And so, this is your fate.

The voice speaks again, so softly that you barely hear the words . . . "you will sleep now. . . ."

And a billion years begin to pass.

The End

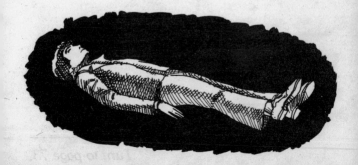

"Well, O.K.," you tell Coleman. "But how are you going to stall him?"

Coleman cocks his head to one side and winks at you. "Just leave that to me."

The two of you return to Bru, who springs out from behind the plum trees.

"Are we ready to go?" he asks.

"I'll need about ten minutes," says Coleman. "My car battery is dead, but I got a friend who owns a garage down the road, and he's on his way over with a new one."

For a moment Bru says nothing. Then he curls up into a ball and springs five or six feet into the air. Sparks fly from his fur as he hovers only a few inches in front of Coleman's sunburned nose.

"Your thoughts are louder than your words," says Bru. He drops for a second to the ground and then springs into the air next to you. Looking you in the eye, he says, "I'm disappointed."

"But I haven't said anything," you say.

"Sometimes," says Bru, "it's a lie to say nothing."

Without another word, he rolls himself up and begins to spin like a top. Suddenly the fast-moving, blurred shape hurtles over the sand dune, and Bru is gone.

You look at Coleman. He stands, head bowed, kicking up little clouds of sand. A moment later you hear the sound of screeching brakes. Glancing toward the road you see two men jumping out of a truck. One of them is carrying a TV camera. They run toward you. Coleman stands looking at them, arms outstretched.

There's nothing to do now but to find your way home. You've missed your chance to make $10,000 fast. Worse than that, you've lost a friend you can never replace. At least you've learned quite a bit—on *UFO 54-40* and right here on Earth.

The End

You deliver your threat.

Nothing happens. Kim Lee puts her hand on your arm. "I don't think you should have said what you did. . . ."

You start to reply, but instantly your eyes are blinded by a blazing yellow light—the last thing that happens to you, and to every other creature on board the *UFO 54-40*.

The End

"Don't worry," says Mopo. "I know what to do. I will go with the Russians."

"Don't go with the Russians," you say.

"I thought you said I can trust human beings," says Mopo.

"But the Russians might try to use you against America," the captain says.

"And, if I am in America, the Russians may think that the Americans will use me against them!"

"But *we* would only ask you to help in the cause of peace," you say.

"That's what they will say, too," says Mopo. "But tell me, do you think I will be for peace?"

"I do," you say. The captain nods his agreement.

Go on to page 92.

"If the Russians are more for war," Mopo says, "and America is more for peace, and I am for peace, then it is better for peace that I go with the Russians, because, if I am with you, it will make them very anxious—so anxious that they might start a war. But, if I am with the Russians, I can guide them toward peace."

By now, the Russian sub is alongside the trawler. Neither you nor the captain can change Mopo's decision to go with them. Soon afterward, the sub submerges with Mopo aboard, leaving you standing by the rail, staring out at the sea.

You're puzzled at Mopo's decision. It almost seems as if he turned against you. On the other hand, you reflect, Mopo may understand Earth people better than you do.

The End

The moment you ask to be returned home, you hear these words in your brain:

YOU ASK US TO BE KIND, BUT KIND-NESS HAS NOTHING TO DO WITH BEING A U-TY.

The U-TY reply chills you to the bone. But you have little time to think about it. The glowing U-TY forms blend into a yellowish mist that slowly darkens into blackness, and you can no longer see, hear, touch, or smell. The darkness and the air of the chamber thicken and close in, and you know nothing but the hope that your life may begin again . . . in a billion years.

The End

Slowly, you awaken. The terrible pressure of the acceleration is gone. The chamber is brightly lit. The air smells fresh and sweet, like a newly mown meadow in spring. Real sunlight and cool air stream through an opening at the end of the chamber. Kim Lee is already standing there, looking out. She turns and beckons. You spring to your feet, and stumble from the force of gravity.

From the opening, you look down at a cornfield about thirty feet beneath you. This incredible machine from a distant planet has obeyed your command. It has taken you through a hundred thousand miles of space. Now it hovers silently only thirty feet in the air. Its great computers seem to know everything—except that, maybe, thirty feet is too far for you to jump.

"Look!" Kim Lee is pointing to the far edge of the field. You had already noticed a herd of cows grazing in the adjoining pasture, but now a man and a boy are running toward you. They stop about fifty feet away, afraid to come closer. Then a small pickup truck lurches over the rise. A man and a woman get out and stare at the sight before them.

Go on to page 96.

"What should we do now?" asks Kim Lee.

But you are lost in thought. You're only dimly aware of her question, and of the men, women, children, and barking dogs now assembling at the edge of the field. You barely hear the police siren in the distance.

You are thinking how strange it is that the all-powerful U-TY masters have evaporated like a mist in the morning sun. And that, when a ship from outer space finally lands, *you are on it.*

Turn to page 116.

"Is there something we can do with these computers?" you ask Angus. "The U-TY seem to have lost control."

But even as you speak, the computers flash and pulsate. Within their electronic brains inconsistent programs must be battling for supremacy. One computer rumbles a moment, then seems to shut down, except for a single flashing red light.

"What's happening?" you ask.

"I don't know," Angus replies. "I don't know what . . ."

But his words are lost in the roar of escaping air, as the whole ship splits open, hurling you, Angus, all the other captives, and the U-TY masters themselves out into the cold black emptiness of space.

The End

"I am the person missing from the Concorde," you say into the mike.

There is a long pause. You stare at your watch. Minutes seem like hours as you wonder—is it time for your life to end?

Three minutes have gone by. Nothing has happened!

Then, "This is NASA; do you read us?"

"Yes!"

"We have obtained computer verification of your identity. We know you were the passenger missing from the Concorde. Your space vessel was designated *UFO 54-40*. We will launch a shuttle to you within seventy-two hours. Don't try to work the controls. The top scientists in the United States are being summoned now. We're going to bring *UFO 54-40* down to Earth."

Kim Lee is jumping up and down. Grinning, she asks, "Will you visit me in China?"

"I sure will!"

The End

Soon after you order the U-TY to reverse course once again and head to Earth, warning lights show that some of the circuits are overheating.

A voice speaks out: *"You-have-made-an-error. You-are-the-master. The-master-cannot-be-in-error. Paradox . . . paradox. . . ."*

The computer begins to vibrate. From somewhere in the star drive, a grinding, whining noise, ascending in pitch, assaults your ear.

"Cancel my last order," you shout. "Proceed to Alara."

"Paradox," drones the computer. *"Double paradox!"*

A shower of sparks floods the room. You throw up your arms to shield your eyes, but you and all the others on board exist for only a moment more—as a brilliant flash of white light.

The End

You walk up to Coleman and look him in the eye. "I can't go along with that. It's not honest, it's not nice, and it's stupid."

Coleman flushes with anger. "C'mon, you got to be out of your mind. You're not going to throw away ten grand!"

But you are already running up the sand dune, calling Bru. He springs from behind a clump of beach plum trees.

"Coleman has called a TV station," you say. "They're on their way here to film you!"

Bru floats toward you. Touching your hand, he says, "Thank you, friend. I will never forget you."

Then, rolling into a furry ball, he spins around so rapidly that soon all you see of him is a bundle of electric sparks that quickly fade, leaving nothing behind.

A week later you are walking near your home when you feel a strange, tingling sensation. You turn and see Bru hovering nearby. Nestling against you like a friendly cat, he says, "Hello, I came to visit for a while."

The End

You did not make a choice, or follow any direction, but now, somehow, you are descending from space—approaching a great, glistening sphere. It is *Ultima*—the planet of paradise. As your ship slowly and gently descends, you look down on a meadow filled with flowers. Beyond them white-capped mountains tower above hills of golden green and smoky blue. Before you lies a crystal city, adorned by sparkling lakes and flowering trees.

Your ship glides to a landing, and a portal slides open. The air smells as fresh and cool as a pine forest. Music fills your ears. Hundreds of people are waiting to greet you—the most beautiful and friendly people you have ever seen. Their skin is dark olive and their large eyes are as green as spring grass. Children run forward. They hand you garlands of flowers. A man and a woman, each wearing golden wreaths in their hair, walk toward you, their arms outstretched.

"Welcome to *Ultima*," says the woman. "My name is Elinka."

"Welcome!" says the man. "My name is Arkam. You have reached the planet of joy and beauty. All our treasures are yours to share with us. All of us here are your friends forever."

Turn to page 102, then 103, then 104.

Taking your hand, Elinka says, "But no land can be paradise if you can never leave it. So you shall always be able to return home whenever you wish—in a flash of time."

"Thank you, thank you," you exclaim. "I never dreamed I would ever find a place like this, or even that it could exist!"

"As you can see, there is such a place after all," says Arkam, "though very few from Earth's universe ever reach it."

"No one can *choose* to visit *Ultima*," says Elinka. "Nor can you get here by following directions. It was a miracle you got here, but that is perfectly logical, because *Ultima* is a miracle itself."

The End

"Let's try to escape," you say.

It takes Angus only a few minutes to find the portal leading to the shuttlecraft. At his touch, the wall opens, revealing a sleek saucer-shaped vehicle.

"It really looks like a flying saucer!" you exclaim.

"That's not a coincidence," says Angus. "It's the most efficient shape for a spacecraft."

In a moment the two of you are seated in the cockpit. "We are lucky, indeed," Angus says. "This craft is controlled automatically. Watch."

Instantly, the craft catapults into space, then veers toward Earth. Within a few hours, you are looking down at farms and woodland below as the craft rapidly descends, brakes, and seems to float for a few moments before gently setting down in a cornfield. Looking through the side ports, you can see two farmers standing by a pickup truck. They are pointing at you, obviously excited by your arrival.

Go on to page 106.

The hatch opens and you leap to the ground.

"Come on," you call to Angus. "I'll give you a hand."

But the kindly old man shakes his head. "Thanks, but when I was captured 1200 years ago I had only a few years to live. So I'll stay on this ship, where I won't grow any older. Besides, my family and friends died long ago."

You're still holding your hand out toward Angus when the port closes and the craft suddenly and completely disappears, leaving you staring in disbelief at the cornfield where you landed minutes before.

"Hey, what was that?" "Where did you come from?" "Where did that thing go?" the farmers yell as they run toward you.

The End

You decide that pretending to be crazy might only make things worse. You pace back and forth, trying to decide what to do. Suddenly, a wall dissolves. In its place is a large curved window. Through it you can see thousands of stars scattered across the jet-black sky. Rows of computers line the other side of the room. Some of them glow with pulsating blue and pink lights.

The ship seems to be turning, and in a minute or so you can see the blue-white sphere you recognize as your own planet, Earth. An alien creature is hunched over one of the computers. Suddenly it crumples to the floor and shrivels up like a dead spider.

Go on to page 108.

Angus is standing beside you; he beckons you closer. His eyes glitter with excitement. "There's an emergency. The computers have a paradox they cannot resolve. That creature did it. It must have been trying to take over the ship." Angus points to the fallen alien. "Some defense mechanism of the U-TY killed it."

He turns away and studies symbols appearing on a display screen. "Our new course will take us near the Earth. There's a shuttlecraft on board this ship. We might be able to take it before the computers resolve the paradox. If the U-TY detect us, they will send us to Somo—to sleep for a billion years."

"Shall we try to escape?"

If you try to escape with Angus on the shuttlecraft, turn to page 105.

If you try to think of something else, turn to page 97.

Slowly, you wake up. Your head is spinning. Your body aches. You are still in the spacecraft, but it's bobbing up and down. You look through the portholes. There is water in all directions. You must be on an Earth ocean!

The alien, Mopo, is still next to you. The hatch cover flips open. Water gushes in. Suddenly Mopo springs out into the ocean.

Through the hatch you can see a grimy white fishing trawler. It's only a few hundred yards away. But the spacecraft is sinking fast. There's no time to waste. You take a deep breath and dive through the hatch into the cold, rough sea. A wave smacks you in the face; then Mopo is lifting you on his back—safely above the waves! The trawler has turned toward you. Wet and shivering, you wave frantically. Two fishermen on the front deck are pointing. They wave back.

"I am afraid that Earth people may kill me," Mopo says. "I must hide in the oceans of Earth so as not to be seen by them."

The trawler is slowing to come alongside. One man is getting ready to throw you a rope. *"Is that a dolphin?"* he yells.

"I must dive now," says Mopo.

"Don't! Come with me," you say.

"Can I trust Earth people, or will they harm me?" he asks.

If you tell Mopo that he can trust Earth people, turn to page 20.

If you tell Mopo that you cannot promise that he will be well treated, turn to page 21.

During the first few days of your voyage home, you learn how to activate the display screens. With the ship's powerful radio telescope, you pick up transmissions from other civilizations. The U-TY instruments bring you in touch with all the wonders of the universe.

But all is not well. Incu seems to be growing smaller. "What is happening, Incu?" you ask.

"I am losing molecules," he replies in a thin, weak voice. "That is what happens to our people when we lose our will to live."

You realize that Incu will die unless you change course to his home planet. Should you order the U-TY to turn back to Alara to save Incu, or should you just try to forget about him?

*If you order the U-TY to head for Alara,
turn to page 42.*

*If you allow the ship to continue on to Earth,
turn to page 43.*

You awaken, dazed and shaken.

"We're on Earth!" Bru cries.

Looking through the open port, you can see that the craft has landed on a sand dune a few hundred feet from a shoreline. The air is warm. The salt air smells good.

Bru stretches his limbs and tests his footing on the sandy ground.

"Can you move all right in Earth gravity?" you ask.

By way of an answer, Bru curls up into a ball and rolls up to the top of a dune. You follow slowly—still shaky after your escape.

"There's an Earth person!" Bru points toward a pot-bellied man, standing by the water's edge, staring out to sea. His surf-casting rod is planted in the sand nearby.

"I'll ask him where we are," you say.

If you take Bru along, turn to page 69.

If you tell Bru to wait, turn to page 67.

You are sitting in your room at home, feeling very strange. What's happened? You remember having boarded the Concorde bound for France, sitting in a seat next to a white-haired man, then . . .

Reaching into your pocket, you pull out a pebble about the size and shape of a watermelon seed. Why is it so heavy? You turn it over and over in your hand, then toss it at the wastebasket.

It's just a matter of luck whether it lands in the wastebasket or not. You have about a fifty-fifty chance.

*Does it go in or not? Turn to either page 41
OR page 50.*

116

For the next hour, you and Kim Lee sit at the doorway of your spacecraft, looking out over the field, watching the crowds gathering, the police roping off a football-field-sized area around you, a police helicopter landing, then army helicopters, TV crews and trucks, fire engines, then army trucks. Finally, even a tank!

"Are they going to shoot at us?" asks Kim Lee.

"They are afraid of aliens," you answer, "but I don't think they'll shoot us. I hope they'll bring a ladder and let us down. Everyone will watch it on TV. Scientists will question us and study this ship so that Earth people can build one like it."

Kim Lee listens intently as you talk. Then she says, "I'm eager to see Earth again and see my country, but I'll miss this ship, because for 475 years it's been my home!"

"Will you miss the U-TY masters?" you ask.

Kim Lee shakes her head. "The U-TY had no more intelligence—no more soul—than slimy, gray snails."

"But they built this miraculous spaceship," you say.

"It is miraculous," she replies, "like a beautiful sea shell left by a slimy, gray snail."

The End

You talk with Kim Lee for a long time. Somehow you feel sure that she and you will be good friends. "Is there any chance for us to escape?" you finally ask.

Kim Lee places a hand on your shoulder. "We are like butterflies in a net—captured by the U-TY masters. Soon, very soon, the *Rakma* will leave the Earth for its home planet, Ra, your new home, hundreds of light-years away. We shall never see Earth again."

"I've got to get out of here," you cry. "I want to meet the U-TY masters. Maybe they will listen to me."

Kim Lee shrugs. "I could show you how to come face to face with the U-TY. I must warn you, though—no one who has tried it has ever returned."

If you decide to meet the U-TY face-to-face, turn to page 38.

If you decide to leave Kim Lee and explore elsewhere in the ship, turn to page 8.

The shapes float toward you, and, before you can retreat a single step, you feel the strange, tingling sensation of their electrifying touch.

> YOUR LOGIC IS TRUE.
> YOU ARE NOT MEANT
> FOR SOMO OR THE ZOO.

With these words the shapes fade into a thin yellow mist that arises about them. You feel tired, but, instead of falling asleep, you rise to another level of wakefulness, so that now, somehow, you find yourself right where you are this minute— reading a book!

The End

ABOUT THE AUTHOR

A graduate of Princeton University and Columbia Law School, *EDWARD PACKARD* lives in New York City, where he is a practicing lawyer. Mr. Packard conceived of the idea for the Choose Your Own Adventure™ series in the course of telling bedtime stories to his children, Caroline, Andrea, and Wells.

ABOUT THE ILLUSTRATOR

PAUL GRANGER is a prize-winning illustrator and painter.

CHOOSE
YOUR OWN
ADVENTURE

You'll want all the books in the exciting *Choose Your Own Adventure* series offering you hundreds of fantasy adventures without ever leaving your chair. Each book takes you through an adventure—under the sea, in a space colony, on a volcanic island—in which you become the main character. What happens next in the story depends on the choices *you* make and *only you* can decide how the story ends!

☐	20892	THE CAVE OF TIME #1 Edward Packard	$1.75
☐	20979	JOURNEY UNDER THE SEA #2 R. A. Montgomery	$1.75
☐	20949	BY BALLOON TO THE SAHARA #3 D. Terman	$1.75
☐	20891	SPACE AND BEYOND #4 R. A. Montgomery	$1.75
☐	14009	THE MYSTERY OF CHIMNEY ROCK #5 Edward Packard	$1.75
☐	20913	YOUR CODE NAME IS JONAH #6 Edward Packard	$1.75
☐	20980	THE THIRD PLANET FROM ALTAIR #7 Edward Packard	$1.75
☐	20982	DEADWOOD CITY #8 Edward Packard	$1.75
☐	20912	WHO KILLED HARLOWE THROMBEY? #9 Edward Packard	$1.75
☐	20983	THE LOST JEWELS OF NABOOTI #10 R. A. Montgomery	$1.75
☐	22620	MYSTERY OF THE MAYA #11 R. A. Montgomery	$1.75
☐	20197	INSIDE UFO 54-40 #12 Edward Packard	$1.75
☐	20529	THE ABOMINABLE SNOWMAN #13 R. A. Montgomery	$1.75
☐	22515	THE FORBIDDEN CASTLE #14 Edward Packard	$1.75
☐	22541	HOUSE OF DANGER #15 R. A. Montgomery	$1.95